LOUDMOUTH GEORGE and the BIG RACE

LOUDMOUTH GEORGE and the BIG RACE

BURNETT

NANCY ★ CARLSON

Carolrhoda Books, Inc. / Minneapolis

For runners everywhere and to fitness for everyone

This book is available in two editions:
Library binding by Carolrhoda Books, Inc., a division of Lerner Publishing Group
Soft cover by First Avenue Editions, an imprint of Lerner Publishing Group
241 First Avenue North
Minneapolis, MN 55401 U.S.A.

Website address: www.carolrhodabooks.com

Library of Congress Cataloging-in-Publication Data

Carlson, Nancy L.
    Loudmouth George and the big race / Nancy Carlson.
      p.   cm.
    Summary: George brags, procrastinates, and offers excuses instead of training for the big race—much to his later embarrassment.
    ISBN: 1–57505–673–9 (lib. bdg. : alk. paper)
    ISBN: 1–57505–724–7 (pbk. : alk. paper)
    [1. Rabbits—Fiction. 2. Racing—Fiction. 3. Excuses—Fiction.] I. Title.
PZ7.C21665Lm 2004
  [E]—dc22   2003023366

Manufactured in the United States of America
1 2 3 4 5 6 – JR – 09 08 07 06 05 04

"Look!" said Harriet. "There's going to be a two-mile race. I'm going to enter."

"Me too," said Ralph. "How about you, George?"

"Sure," said George. "Two miles will be a breeze for *me*."

"I'm going to start training right now," said Harriet.

"Me too," said Ralph. "How about you, George?"

"You guys can train all you like," said George.
"I'm going to beat you anyway. I'll start *my* training
tomorrow."

That night, George went to bed early. He set his alarm clock for five o'clock.

"Professional runners run early in the morning," he said.

But when five o'clock came, George just couldn't get up.

"*Smart* professional runners run later," he mumbled, and he went back to sleep.

It was noon when George finally came downstairs.
"Going running, George?" asked his mother.
"In the midday sun?" said George. "Do you
want me to get heatstroke? I'll run tonight, when
it's cooler."

After supper, George got interested in a television show. "I can start training tomorrow," he said.

In the morning, George saw Harriet jog by.

"She looks terrible," said George. "I'd better get out there and show her how it's done."

But when George got downstairs, his mother was making pancakes.

"It'll wait till after breakfast," said George.

After breakfast, George was too full to run.
"I'm going to really train hard after supper," he
said. "I may even run ten miles."

That night after supper, Uncle Chuck stopped by.
"Who wants to go to the movies with me?" he
asked.
"I do!" said George.
On their way, Harriet passed them.

"Training for the big race?" said Uncle Chuck.

"I sure am," said Harriet. "I can run a mile and a half now. How about you, George?"

"You bet," said George, "and I don't even start my *real* training until tomorrow."

The next day, it rained.

The day after that, George had swimming lessons.
The day after that, it was too windy to run.
The day after that, it was too cold.
The day after that, it was too hot.

Finally, the day of the big race arrived.

"Boy, am I scared!" said Harriet.

"Not me," said George. "A two-mile race is nothing for *me*—just a walk in the park.

The gun fired, and the racers were off.

George ran out fast—ahead of everyone.

"Just like I thought," he said to himself. "I'm in first place already."

After about two blocks, George began to feel a
little out of breath.

First, Harriet passed him.

Then Ralph.

By the end of the first mile, almost everyone had passed him. George felt really tired.

Finally, he made it to the finish line . . .

just in time to see Harriet get her trophy. She took first place.

George sat down under a tree to catch his breath. "I've been looking all over for you," said Harriet. "How did you do?"

"Uh ... er ... not very well," George admitted. "My shoes were too tight."

"Don't feel too bad, George," said Harriet.
"There's a three-mile race in two weeks. I'm going to
start training this afternoon. Want to run with me?"

"This afternoon?" said George. "Gee, I don't
think so, Harriet. I'm kind of tired. . . ."

"I'll start training tomorrow."